# TALL STORIES

## A BOOK OF GIANTS

### BY JOHN PATIENCE

# The Quarrelsome Giants or A Prince of Pigs

Farmer was driving his cart home from market. In the back was a pig which he had failed to sell. What was he going to tell his wife? They had no money left – selling the pig had been their only hope of surviving through the approaching winter. It was not surprising that he had failed to sell the pig, for it was an exceptionally poor looking animal, all skin and bones!

As the farmer was driving along the road he passed by the mouth of a cave and heard a terrible, fierce argument going on inside it. The two voices sounded like thunder and could only belong to a couple of giants. Naturally, the farmer was very much afraid, but it occurred to him that the giants might be interested in buying his pig. After all, what did he have to lose by asking them – only his life and it really wasn't much of a life, scratching around on his miserable little farm. So, mustering up all his courage, the farmer (whose name incidentally was Olaf) climbed down from his cart, put the pig on its lead and gingerly stepped into the cave.

The two giants who (to get all the introductions over with), were brothers named Grumble and Rumble, stopped arguing and eyed the farmer suspiciously. "What do you want?" rumbled Grumble. "And what's that there article you've got with you?" grumbled Rumble. "I'm just a poor farmer," replied Olaf, doffing his hat. "But I happen to own this article, which is actually a pig. A beautiful animal, as I'm sure you will agree. I was wondering if either of you two fine gentlemen would like to buy him from me?" Grumble and Rumble laughed fit to bust. "Buy him from you!" roared Grumble. "We don't buy things, we just takes 'em. And who's going to stop us taking this here pig, eh? Not you, I'm sure." "Quite right," said Olaf, realising that he was in a tricky position. "Buy him? Did I say that? Silly me! He's a present. Of course he is. Take him, please do."

But as he spoke the seed of a plan began to grow in the farmer's mind. "However, this is not an ordinary pig," he continued. "He's really a Prince of Pigs and I wouldn't want him to be eaten by just any old giant. I think that the stronger of the two of you should have him." "That sounds fair enough," said Rumble. "You mean me." "No, he doesn't," growled Grumble, "I'm the stronger." "We'll soon see about that!" shouted Rumble, preparing to knock his brother into the middle of next week. "Well now, perhaps a sort of contest should be held to decide the matter," suggested Olaf, soothingly. "Good idea," agreed Grumble. "All right," said Rumble. "I'll win, anyway!"

"Set me a task. I can do anything you can think of," boasted Grumble, flexing his immense muscles. "Very well," said the farmer. "You see that forest over there? Do you think you could clear it away?" "No sooner said than done," said Grumble and it was very nearly true, for Grumble set to with a will. He uprooted the trees with his bare hands and, one after another, tossed them high over the mountain. "Well, what do you think of that?" he asked.

"Absolutely marvellous!" said the farmer. "The pig's mine then," said the giant. "I could do with a bit of a snack after all that hard work."

"Hold on a minute," growled Rumble. "I haven't had my turn yet. Set me a task, Farmer. I can do ten times better than my weakling brother." Well, the cunning old farmer rubbed his chin and scratched his head for a while, and then he said, "I don't suppose you could build a palace over there where your brother pulled up the forest, could you?"

"Couldn't I though!" blustered Rumble. "Just you watch me!" Then, while the farmer looked on in amazement, the giant set to work and, believe it or not, in the twinkling of an eye he had built the most magnificent palace on the face of the earth! "There you are," he said, dusting off his hands. "No problem. The pig is mine." "No it's not!" bellowed his brother. "It's mine. I'm the strongest." "Of course you're not," mocked Rumble. "You're a weed." "I'll teach you a thing or two," thundered Grumble. And the next moment the two monstrosities were locked in a terrible battle.

The fight went on and on all day long, with first one giant getting the upper hand and then the other, until finally, as night was falling, Grumble got the definite advantage. He lifted Rumble up off his feet and, with all his might, he threw him into the air. But Rumble was as fast as lightning and he managed to grab hold of his brother's beard, pulling him up with him. So away they both flew, high into the starry sky, up and up and over the moon. And where they landed I do not know, for they were never seen again.

As for the crafty farmer, he returned to the giants' cave, where he found a hoard of gold and silver and precious stones which he promptly loaded up onto his cart. Then, with the Prince of Pigs sitting up on top of it, away he went, along the winding road, up over the mountain and at last he arrived back home. And there was his dear wife, standing beside the farm house. It had been completely flattened by a tree which his wife assured him had fallen straight out of the sky.

Well, the farmer didn't worry too much about his demolished farm house. He and his wife went to live in the beautiful palace which he had tricked the giant Rumble into building. And what with the giants' treasure, they were very well off to the end of their days. "But what happened to the pig?" you might ask. Well, now he was really the Prince of Pigs for Olaf bought him a real crown and an ermine robe and gave him lots and lots of lovely food to eat so that, in the end, he became quite porky!

# When Giants get Sneezes

 hen giants get sneezes and
Coughs and diseases,
They ought to stay home
And keep warm.
For gigantic sneezes
Can blow down our treeses
And whip up a terrible storm!

# The Giant Who Couldn't Sleep

There was once a village where, as night began to fall, people became afraid and would hide themselves away in their houses, bolt their doors, shutter their windows and crawl under their beds. There was a very good reason for this peculiar behaviour, for every evening a great giant would come striding down from the mountains and stomp around the village streets. Over his shoulder he carried an enormous club and upon his face he wore a terrible scowl. "He's looking for someone to gobble up for his supper," mothers would whisper to their children. "Be quiet while he passes."

Every night it was the same story, until one night it was different. As the giant was wandering around the deserted streets he came upon a little boy sitting in a tree. He had climbed up to get his toy aeroplane which had got stuck in the branches, and now he couldn't get down. The little boy, whose name was Ben, trembled with fear when he saw the giant lumbering towards him. He covered his eyes and peeped out between his fingers and saw one of the giant's monstrous great hands reaching out to grab him. Then, to his surprise, he found himself being very gently lifted up out of the tree and set safely down upon the ground.

"Are you g-g-going to eat me?" stammered Ben. "No! Of course not," rumbled the giant. "I'm a vegetarian, and besides, you seem to be a nice little boy. Perhaps we can be friends. Look, here's your aeroplane." The giant carefully picked the toy out of the tree and sent it gliding down to the little boy.

"Everyone says you're fierce," said the boy, looking up at the giant, his eyes round with wonder, "but you're not at all, are you?" "Certainly not!" replied the giant, rather affronted. "Then why do you prowl around the village every night?" "I can't sleep," sighed the giant, and the sigh was such a big heavy sigh that it almost blew Ben off his feet. "Not a wink. And I get so lonely. So I come down into the village looking for company." "Have you tried counting sheep?" asked Ben. "Yes, I have," said the giant, "but I'm not too good at counting. I get up to seven, then I'm not sure what comes next. Is it nine or twelve?" "Fifteen, I think," suggested Ben. "But I think I know a way to make you sleep. Can you take me home? There is something I have to get." "Of course," said the giant, and he picked up the little boy and sat him upon his shoulder and off they went.

Ben's mother and father were overjoyed to see him back safe and sound, but they were very wary of his new friend, the giant. "Oh dear! He's sure to eat us all up," whispered his mother. "Don't be silly. He's a vegetarian," said Ben. Then, calling over his shoulder, "Don't go away giant. I'll be back in a minute," he ran off to his bedroom. In a few minutes he reappeared, carrying a large book. "I shan't be long," he said reassuringly to his mother and father. "I'm just off to my friend's house." Ben's bewildered parents stood on their doorstep and watched as he climbed up onto the giant's shoulder. "Good-bye!" he called. "See you later." Then the giant lumbered away into the moonlight, his great footsteps shaking the ground beneath him.

The giant climbed higher and higher, picking his way up the winding mountain path and leaving the village so far below them that it looked like a tiny toy. Up and up they went until, at last, they reached an enormous wooden door set into the rock. "Here we are," said the giant, opening the door and stepping inside. "It's not much, but it's home." As a matter of fact, it looked very nice and was a lot more comfortable than you might imagine a giant's cave to be.

Ben hurried the giant along and soon he was climbing into his gigantic bed, a bed big enough for a couple of elephants! "Well," he said, yawning, "what's your plan, Ben?" "It's simple," replied Ben, sitting himself down on the bedside table, under the light of the candle. "I'm going to read you a bedtime story. You'll be off to sleep in no time." And he began to read.

"Once upon a time, long ago, there was a ..." Ben was right. In no time at all the giant's eyelids grew heavy and he fell into a deep sleep. Then Ben crept quietly out of the cave and made his way home. From then on, Ben read to the giant every night and for a while everything was fine. Then one night everyone in the village was woken by a terrible shout. "Help! Save me, save me!" It was the giant's voice booming down from the mountain. Ben quickly put on his dressing gown and, taking a lamp, climbed up the winding path to the giant's cave. There he found his friend hiding under the bedclothes. "What's the matter?" asked the little boy. "It's the monster. It came to get me!" said the giant, peeping out from under the sheets. "Rubbish!" scoffed Ben. "There's no such thing as monsters. You were having a nightmare." Soon Ben settled his friend down, read him another story and went home. But the next night and the next night and every night for a week the giant woke the village with his shouting. His nightmares were becoming a big problem!

No one knew what to do, then Ben had another brilliant idea. A giant teddy bear! It involved a great deal of work. The farmer brought a cartload of wool to stuff it with. The tailor provided the furry material and Ben's mother and her friends worked until their fingers were sore from stitching. Then, when it was finished, four strong men were needed to help Ben carry the teddy up the mountain – one for each arm and one for each leg!

"Now, Giant," said Ben. "You take this teddy to bed with you and you will never have another bad dream. I know. I take my ted to bed with me and I never have nightmares. Teddies are magic, you see, my mother told me so." Well, the giant was happy now. He snuggled up with his teddy bear and listened to Ben reading him his bedtime story, and fell fast asleep. A sleep with no monsters in it!

"Well, that's that," said Ben, climbing into his own bed. "We can all get some sleep now." "Yes," said his mother as she tucked him in. "It will be very peaceful." But they were both wrong, for no sooner had they spoken, than a new noise came rumbling down from the mountain. It was deafening! It was the sound of the giant snoring, and it shook every bed and rattled every window in the village. But there was nothing anyone could do about that, not even Ben. So, from that day on, they all had to go to bed with cotton wool in their ears!

# My Best Friend

My best friend is a giant.
He's bigger than our house.
He's stronger than an elephant,
But quiet as a mouse.
No-one else can see him,
He's invisible, you see,
But he pushes me on the garden swing
And helps me climb the tree.
Sometimes he tells me stories,
As I sit in the palm of his hand,
Of fabulous beasts,
Of fairyland feasts,
Of a mystical, magical land.
But it's a shame when it starts to rain.
He often starts to cry,
'Cause he's too big to come indoors
And we have to say goodbye.

# The Greedy Giant and The Miserable Princess

**P**rincess Priscilla was the most beautiful girl in the world. She wore fine clothes, rode around the town in a golden carriage and had scores of servants who pandered to her every whim. Now, you might think that all this would have made her happy, but not a bit of it. The princess was extremely discontented and somehow she managed to make everyone else feel the same way. "I wish something would happen," she would say. "Life is so boring. I wish someone would make me laugh." Well, everyone DID try to make her laugh, but it was no use. She was so miserable that she could reduce the jolliest jester to tears in next to no time. Eventually, the king grew so exasperated with his daughter that he decided to get rid of her by marrying her off to the first prince who could so much as make her smile.

Messengers were sent out from the palace with invitations to all the princes thereabouts to attend a great feast, at which Priscilla would choose a husband.

The day of the feast dawned and the tables in the banqueting hall groaned under the weight of the most succulent, mouth-watering food you can possibly imagine. But before they began to eat, the princes, all seven of them, were introduced to the Princess Priscilla. Unfortunately the princess was looking especially beautiful that day and all the princes lost their hearts to her. But, try as they might, they could not make her smile and they were all rejected. "They are all so dull," sighed the miserable princess.

At that moment things were livened up considerably by a terrible roar and the sound of thunderous footsteps approaching. The great door burst open and in strode the fiercest giant you ever clapped eyes on. He had heard about the feast and was not one to miss the chance of a good meal. Without more ado he sat himself down and began to eat everything in sight. Soon he had polished off the lot! Then, wiping his mouth with the back of his hand, he roared,

"Bring me more food or I'll eat the lot of you." And by the look of his gigantic teeth that would have given him no trouble at all! The servants were sent scurrying down to the kitchen and the fear that they themselves might be the giant's next meal made them double quick about bringing back everything they could find. "This will do very nicely, for the moment," said the giant, talking (as giants often do) with his mouth full.

The giant finished off his meal then fell fast asleep. When he awoke a little while later he was feeling rather peckish. "Bring me more food!" he bellowed, "or ..." "We know," sighed the king. "Or you'll eat the lot of us." But now the king's larders were empty and food had to be fetched up from the town, by the cart load.

The greedy giant knew when he was well off and decided to stay in the palace for a while. The days passed and his appetite only seemed to grow larger. Cheeses as big as millstones were brought to him. Loaves as large as haystacks were baked for him and, in short, every scrap of food from miles around was delivered up to the giant. Until at last, there was hardly a crumb of food left in the whole kingdom and even the mice were starving and as thin as matchsticks.

Realising that something must be done, the king issued a proclamation that anyone who could rid the kingdom of the giant would be granted the beautiful Princess Priscilla's hand in marriage and he wouldn't even have to make her smile or be a prince! The princess herself was not too pleased with this idea, but she was as tired as anyone else of the giant and so she agreed to the plan.

Now, there was a boy who worked in the king's kitchens and he had long been in love with Priscilla. He realised at once that this was his big chance. He promised the king that if he could supply him with the ingredients to make a giant pie, then he could do the trick. Well, one way or another (though, as I have said, there was little food left in the land), the ingredients for the pie were found and the kitchen boy got to work with them. All night long he slaved, stirring up a great, gooey pan of treacle, rolling out an enormous sheet of pastry and finally baking the pie. In the morning, with the help of a number of other servants, he carried the pie up to the banqueting hall and set it before the giant.

The giant's greedy eyes almost popped out of his head when he saw the pie and, opening up his mouth as wide as a cave, he sunk his terrible teeth into it and began to chew, and chew, and chew. The pie was chewy. More than chewy, it was gluey. So gluey that soon the puzzled giant found that his teeth were stuck together. Try as he might, he could not get them apart. He mumbled and grumbled, contorted his face into the most peculiar shapes and turned bright red. He was the funniest thing anyone had ever seen and they all exploded into fits of laughter. Then a most peculiar sound split the air. It was horrible! Everyone looked around to see where the sound was coming from and, to their amazement, they found it was the princess. She was laughing, but what a laugh! How could such a terrible laugh come from such a beautiful person? Priscilla laughed until she wept, pointing her finger at the unfortunate giant and exclaiming, "He's so funny. Just look at him!" Now the giant couldn't get his teeth apart, he couldn't eat anyone and soon he became so embarrassed that he stumbled out of the palace, ran away into the hills and was never seen again.

And did the kitchen lad marry the beautiful Princess Priscilla? No, I'm afraid he didn't. Her horrible laughter had completely put him off. It had put everyone off. But then Priscilla didn't mind. "They're all boring, anyway," she told herself. And maybe they were. And maybe they weren't.